D1315791

I'M
CALLING
MOLLY

*For Leonard, David, Jonathan, and the real Rebekah,
and for Trinidad, where the sand dragons play. J.K.*

For Becca, my neighbor, with love. I.T.

Text © 1990 by Jane Kurtz.
Illustrations © 1990 by Irene Trivas.
Published in 1990 by Albert Whitman & Company,
5747 West Howard Street, Niles, Illinois 60648.
Published simultaneously in Canada
by General Publishing, Limited, Toronto.
10 9 8 7 6 5 4 3 2 1

Library of Congress Cataloging-in-Publication Data
Kurtz, Jane.
    I'm calling Molly / Jane Kurtz;
pictures by Irene Trivas.
        p.   cm.
    Summary: Four-year-old Christopher, who has just
learned to use the telephone, calls Molly using
various ploys to persuade her to play with him, but
she is busy with another friend.
ISBN 0-8075-3468-4
    [1. Telephone—Fiction.   2. Friendship—Fiction.]
I. Trivas, Irene, ill.   II. Title.
PZ7.K9626Im   1990   89-35873
[E]—dc20   CIP
                                                AC

Jane Kurtz

I'M CALLING MOLLY

PICTURES BY Irene Trivas

ALBERT WHITMAN & COMPANY · NILES, ILLINOIS

My name is Christopher, and I live in a green house where dragons used to roost under the roof.

My best friend's name is Molly, and she lives next doo

Molly has hair as red as lava
from a volcano. She's the one
who told me about the dragons
at our house. Molly knows
everything about dragons.

Last week, I learned Molly's telephone
number. Now I can call Molly whenever I want,
and I'm calling Molly.
555-8339.
"Hello?" Molly says.

"Hello," I say. "Come on over. I need to talk to you about making gorilla stew."

"I can't come over," Molly says. "I'm making gorilla stew with Rebekah."

"Goodbye," I say.

I go into the kitchen where my mom is typing.

I say, "Molly is playing with Rebekah, and she won't play with me."

"Just wait," my mom says. "I'm sure she and Rebekah won't play together forever." She types some more.

I go to the living room
window and look out at Molly's
house.

Just yesterday, Molly pushed me down the sidewalk in my little brother's stroller.

Just yesterday, Molly told me about sand dragons who live in the desert and eat sand bugs and people.

Just yesterday, I played
football with Molly's dog.

Today Molly wouldn't even
let her dog in my yard, even
when I said, "Pretty please
with cupcakes on top."
It's not fair, not fair.

I'm calling Molly.
555-8339.
"Hello," Molly says.
"Hello," I say. "When can you come over? I
think I saw a dragon-wing fossil in the back
yard yesterday. We need to dress up like
explorers and dig it up."

"I can't come over," Molly says. "I'm in the middle of playing dress-up with Rebekah."

"Goodbye," I say.

I go into the kitchen and lean against the table. "Why don't you play with your explorer binoculars?" my mom says.

"You have to have both binoculars," I say. "It's no fun without Molly's binoculars, too."

Molly's back door slams. I
run out onto the porch.

Molly has on high heels and a black wig. Rebekah is wearing a giant hat with a feather.

They march down the sidewalk. When Molly
and Rebekah get to my house, they look up.
"We don't know you," Molly says.

Rebekah giggles. "We never even saw you
before," she says.

They turn around and start marching to Molly's house. I go into my own house and slam the door.

My mom is still typing in the kitchen. "Molly's being mean," I say. "Will you read me a story?" My mom looks at her watch. "Let me finish this," she says. "Give me fifteen minutes."

I look at my arm, but my watch isn't there. Then I remember about Molly and my watch.

I'm calling Molly. 555-8339.
"Hello?" Molly says.
"Hello," I say. "I think I left
my black underwater watch
at your house when we were
making wombat stew. Can you
bring it over?"

"Rebekah has a purple
watch with green numbers,"
Molly says. "I can't come over
because I'm looking at
Rebekah's watch."

"Goodbye," I say.

I go out and sit on the porch swing. After a while, my mom comes and reads my book about desert explorers. The bravest explorer is climbing a gigantic sand dune where anything, even a dragon, might be hiding.

When she's done, I put on my hiking boots.
I sit on the swing and pretend that I'm hunting
for sand dragons. Molly is back home making
stew because she isn't brave enough to hunt
sand dragons.

I hope she tries to make stew out of an elephant, and the elephant stomps on her.

I hope she goes inside a dragon egg and never hatches.

I hope if she does hatch, the dragons eat her up.

I see Rebekah's mom drive up. When she honks, Rebekah runs out the door, waving to Molly.

I sit on the porch with my boots up.

I'm not calling Molly because I'm far away in the desert.

I'm not calling Molly because the sand
dragons will hear me if I make even one
little noise.

I can see Molly through
the window, but I'm not
calling Molly

because Molly's calling me.

ABOUT THE AUTHOR

Jane Kurtz lives in Trinidad, Colorado, with her husband, three children, one cat, and two rabbits. This is her first picture book.

ABOUT THE ILLUSTRATOR

Irene Trivas has written and illustrated *Emma's Christmas* and has illustrated many books for children. *I'm Calling Molly* is her third book for Albert Whitman. Irene lives in West Newbury, Vermont.